Puffin Books

JIMMY TAG-ALONG

BRIAN PATTEN was born in Liverpool. He began writing poetry in school when he was fourteen years old in defiance of a careers officer who had told him to concentrate on getting a job in a factory. At fifteen he began publishing a magazine called *Underdog*, which was the first magazine to publish seriously much of the then 'underground' poetry. Brian Patten has now become a highly successful poet for both adults and children and is a popular performer. His work has been widely anthologized, and he had also written a novel and a stage play for children.

JIMMY
TAG-ALONG

BRIAN PATTEN

ILLUSTRATED BY DAVID MOSTYN

PUFFIN BOOKS

PUFFIN BOOKS

Published by the Penguin Group
Penguin Books Ltd, 27 Wrights Lane, London W8 5TZ, England
Penguin Books USA Inc., 375 Hudson Street, New York, New York 10014, USA
Penguin Books Australia Ltd, Ringwood, Victoria, Australia
Penguin Books Canada Ltd, 10 Alcorn Avenue, Toronto, Ontario, Canada M4V 3B2
Penguin Books (NZ) Ltd, 182–190 Wairau Road, Auckland 10, New Zealand

Penguin Books Ltd, Registered Offices: Harmondsworth, Middlesex, England

First published by Viking Kestrel 1988
Published in Puffin Books 1989
10 9 8 7 6 5 4

Text copyright © Brian Patten, 1988
Illustrations copyright © David Mostyn, 1988
All rights reserved

Printed in England by Clays Ltd, St Ives plc

Jimmy Tag-along

My secret adventures began a few days
after I moved into a new neighbourhood.

Mum said I was not to bother the two
nice old people who lived in the houses that
backed on to our garden.

'The poor dears seem a bit dotty, and you
shouldn't go exhausting them with
questions,' she said.

I was dying to see what was dotty about
them, so I rushed upstairs and looked out
of the top window.

What I saw was fantastic! It was Mrs

Battyhats's and Uncle Elliot's gardens!

That was their names. They told me when I dashed back downstairs and peeped over the garden fence.

'Hello,' said Mrs Battyhats, 'I'm Mrs Battyhats. What's your name?'

'James,' I said.

'That won't do, will it, Uncle Elliot?' said Mrs Battyhats.

'It *is* a bit ordinary,' said Uncle Elliot. 'Little boys should have special secret names.'

Mrs Battyhats was wearing a gigantic hat made entirely of sweets. She picked a wine-gum from it and chewed it thoughtfully.

'We'll call him Gnat,' she said.

'Oh no, you won't,' I said.

'How about Cow-pat then?' she asked.

'Most certainly not,' I said.

'Well, I suppose we could always call you

Wombat, or Rat, or Laundromat. Even Batty would do at a pinch.'

'But why?' I asked.

'Because Batty almost rhymes with hat, and Gnat and Wombat and Rat and Laundromat most certainly do. I'm very fond of anything that rhymes with hat,' she said. 'Except of course bureaucrat.'

'But I'm not at all batty. I'm quite sensible,' I told her.

'How boring it must be to be sensible all the time,' sighed Uncle Elliot.

'I don't like being sensible *all* the time,' I said.

'Then we'll call you Jimmy Tag-along, because you'll be wanting to tag along with us on some of our adventures – won't he, Mrs Battyhats?'

'He most certainly will,' she said.

So that's how I became known as Jimmy

Tag-along, and I tagged along with them on their crazy adventures.

They had to be secret adventures, of course. If Mum and Dad had ever found out what we got up to, they would have been furious. Like everybody else, they thought Uncle Elliot and Mrs Battyhats were just two harmless old people.

No one realized quite how wonderful they were.

Mrs Battyhats and Uncle Elliot didn't seem to care about the things most grown-ups cared about. They never bothered about keeping things tidy or being on time. And they never ever told me off for doing things I shouldn't have done, or complained when I wanted to stay up late or got things muddy.

Before I describe any of our adventures I ought to tell you a bit about my two friends.

Mrs Battyhats

As you will have guessed by her name, Mrs Battyhats was batty. She was the kind of person you'd love to hug (though you could only have hugged one bit of her at a time). She was as tubby as a tub and she had the most fantastic collection of hats in the world.

She had gigantic hats and tiny hats. Hats that looked like helter-skelters and hats that looked like junk yards.

She had a frog hat that croaked, and a bee-hive hat that buzzed, and a hat that was really a cage in which she kept a pet mouse.

She had a hat that had once been a stork's nest (the stork sometimes came back to visit), and a lobster hat that pinched things when she went out shopping, and a vampire-bat hat that was always trying to suck people's blood. (She was told off by policemen when she wore this hat.)

She had hats that smelt of honeysuckle and hats as fresh as waterfalls, hats made of mouth-wateringly scrumptious sweets and floppy, dark hats made out of liquorice.

When she was sad she sometimes wore hats that played sad tunes, and then big, round tears would fall out of her eyes.

But mostly Mrs Battyhats was happy.

Uncle Elliot

Uncle Elliot was good at almost everything. I can't tell you how many things he was good at – there were far too many.

He was a genius at reading maps, for example. And at drawing them. He must have had at least ten thousand maps in his house.

The thing he loved most was exploring, and he didn't mind what he explored.

He explored deserts and jungles and birds' nests and rabbit warrens and boxes full of buttons.

He explored cupboards full of coat-hangers and attics full of spiders and glittering caverns full of ice. He had even explored the moon (twice), or so he told me.

And wherever he went he took along with him his Emergency Bag, which contained a bit of everything.

Uncle Elliot was curious about most things, and I'd never met anyone like him.

He was also a genius at finding things.

Once he found a dragon's tooth (but no dragon).

Once he found a unicorn's horn (but no unicorn).

Once he found a dinosaur's tail (but no dinosaur).

Once he even found a dodo.

That was our very first adventure.

Uncle Elliot and the Dodo

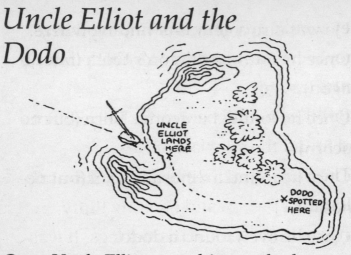

Once Uncle Elliot was shipwrecked on a
desert island for half an hour. While he was
looking for wood to build a new boat and
sail back home, he found a dodo. It was
standing at the edge of a jungle clearing,
nibbling leaves and minding its own
business. When it saw Uncle Elliot it tried to
run away, but Uncle Elliot was too quick
for it.

It was the very last dodo in the world.

If you were to ask a teacher or a professor
the question 'Where can I find a dodo?',

they would probably answer, 'Nowhere. They were all guzzled by terrible pirates centuries ago.'

But they would be wrong. Uncle Elliot had found the very last one.

The dodo was three feet high. It was the colour of a pigeon and had tiny fluffy wings, a huge beak and stout legs. It was also rather silly because, once caught, it never thought of trying to escape. Instead it simply stood around scratching itself and whistling 'Yo ho ho and a bottle of rum'

(which is the song pirates used to sing when they barbecued dodos).

It was one of the strangest birds ever to have lived on the planet.

When Uncle Elliot had finished building his new boat, he wrapped the dodo up carefully in a couple of banana leaves and sailed back home.

The moment he got back he began making a marvellous hutch at the bottom of his garden.

Mrs Battyhats was sitting in her sitting-room, yawning and knitting a night-cap. She heard Uncle Elliot hammering away and peeped out of her window. When she saw the dodo, she decided it would make a perfect hat.

I'll nip over the fence and get it later,' she thought.

And that is exactly what she did.

I was leaning out of the top window at the time, staring at nothing in particular. I was bored and absolutely itching for something exciting to happen, and when I saw Mrs Battyhats climbing over the fence, I couldn't resist shouting down to her, 'What are you up to?'

'Shush,' she said, 'I'm after Uncle Elliot's dodo.'

'He'll be furious,' I whispered.

'Nonsense,' she said. 'I'm sure the dodo

would be much happier sitting on my head
pretending to be a hat than living in a
disgusting old hutch. Just you be quiet,
Jimmy Tag-along.'

I wanted to point out that the hutch was
brand-new and not at all disgusting, but
there was no stopping Mrs Battyhats once
she'd got an idea into her head, specially if
it was an idea to do with hats.

The dodo was quite unaware of her as it stood outside the hutch having a whistle and a scratch.

She sneaked up on it, slyly and slowly at first, but the closer she sneaked, the noisier and more excited she became, and when she couldn't contain her excitement any longer she made a lunge for the bird.
And missed.

The noise of her crashing into the hutch brought Uncle Elliot into the garden.

He found Mrs Battyhats with her behind and left leg sticking out of the hutch, and the rest of her firmly jammed inside.

He was furious, just like I'd said he would be.

He had been sitting in the kitchen, busily designing balloons in which he hoped to float around the moon and back, and when he saw what Mrs Battyhats had been up to, he brought one out.

He dislodged her from the hutch and
after a tremendous struggle tied her to the
balloon. Then, using a cylinder of gas, he
blew the balloon up and let it go.

The balloon floated off into the sky with

Mrs Battyhats wriggling beneath it. I tried
to grab her as she drifted past my window,
but I missed, and soon she was no more
than an angry little dot among the clouds.

She didn't float up to the moon, as Uncle
Elliot had expected, but instead she floated
in a southerly direction at about three
hundred feet. He watched until she had
vanished, and then went back inside to

have a cup of hot chocolate and calm himself down.

I had been watching these ludicrous goings-on in amazement. Don't forget, I had only just moved into the neighbourhood and had not got to know Mrs Battyhats or Uncle Elliot very well, so when Mrs Battyhats floated past my window I was more than a little alarmed.

I knew grown-ups sometimes did crazy things, but tying an old lady to a balloon and sending her floating off across the roof tops seemed a bit much.

I imagined the balloon drifting around the world for ever, with Mrs Battyhats dangling beneath it and being fed the occasional worm by a passing pigeon.

It wasn't a nice thought, so I sneaked downstairs and climbed over the fence into Uncle Elliot's garden.

I tapped on his window and when he opened the back door I said, 'Don't you think you are being a bit cruel?'

He pondered this statement for a few minutes. 'Perhaps I was a teeny weeny bit hasty,' he replied.

The more he pondered, the more he regretted his actions. He decided life would be dull without Mrs Battyhats around.

'I'd better make another balloon and go and look for her,' he sighed.

Instead of going to sleep that night, I helped Uncle Elliot make his best balloon ever.

Beneath it we attached a basket and built a special rudder for steering. When everything was ready Uncle Elliot climbed into the basket.

'Will you hand up the dodo?' he asked. 'I'd better not leave it behind.'

I could understand why he chose not to leave the dodo behind. The chaos in the garden had agitated the bird so much it was whistling 'Yo ho ho and a bottle of rum' at the top of its voice and was threatening to

wake the entire neighbourhood.

When I lifted the bird up, Uncle Elliot could see I was dying to have a ride in the balloon myself and he asked, 'Do you fancy tagging along?'

Did I just! I scrambled in before he could change his mind, and soon we were floating above the city.

The air was sharp and cold and made me tingle, and it was dizzy-making floating so high above the earth.

We looked for her in ruined temples on the tops of mountains. We floated across bright blue seas and burning red deserts. I steered the balloon while Uncle Elliot sat on the edge of the basket looking down through his telescope.

We found Mrs Battyhats early next morning.

We were floating across a jungle and spied her tangled in the branches of a tree above a swamp full of crocodiles. Fortunately the crocodiles were still asleep.

Mrs Battyhats was terribly frightened. She was wriggling and whimpering as quietly as possible and was horrified when she saw the dodo peeping over the side of the basket.

She was convinced it was going to squark and wake the crocodiles, but it seemed happy enough just staring down at them.

The dodo did look puzzled, though.
Perhaps it thought dangling from torn
balloons above a swamp full of crocodiles
was what human beings did for fun.

Uncle Elliot took a rope ladder from his
Emergency Bag. He lowered it from the
balloon, climbed down and tiptoed across
the backs of the sleeping crocodiles.

He was as light as a feather and as quiet
as a dew drop.

Twice the crocs stirred in their sleep, but
he hummed a sleepy tune, so they carried
on snoring and dreaming of breakfast. By
the time they yawned and blinked awake
we had lifted Mrs Battyhats safely aboard
and were drifting back off across the jungle.

For a few moments she grovelled on her
knees and thanked us for rescuing her,
but she soon became her normal
self again.

We were half-way across the Indian
Ocean when the dodo stopped staring over
the side of the basket and began pecking at
my sleeve. At first I thought it was worried
in case Mrs Battyhats attempted to grab it
and stick it on her head again, but I was
wrong.

The dodo had spotted its island down
below and longed to return home.

You can imagine how ashamed everyone felt when the dodo began squarking and imploring to be let go. Uncle Elliot and Mrs Battyhats regretted the bother they had caused and agreed the only decent thing to do was to land on the island and set it free.

And so we did.

We stayed on the island for a couple of hours, drinking fruit juice and eating coconuts, and then we kissed the dodo goodbye and climbed back into the basket.

Before we left, Mrs Battyhats took off her hat, which had been stuck firmly on her head throughout the entire adventure, and gave it to the dodo as a present. The dodo loved it, and hugged it tightly as if it were a friend.

Then the balloon rose, and we were away.

The dodo stayed below, twittering happily as it watched us rise up into the air. Then it gave a sigh of relief and hurried off among the trees, never to be seen again.

'Let's all promise not to tell anyone where the dodo lives,' said Uncle Elliot, 'and then no one can repeat my mistakes.'

'I promise,' said Mrs Battyhats.

'And so do I,' I said, although I had never intended the dodo any harm in the first place.

I snuggled up to Mrs Battyhats for warmth and I must have fallen asleep, because the next thing I knew she was gently shaking me awake and telling me we were home. I looked out of the basket and saw our gardens below us.

It was evening. The birds had stopped singing and the tops of the trees glittered with frost. I was absolutely exhausted. Of course, Mum never realized what I had been up to. She thought I'd simply woken up early and gone on an outing with Mrs Battyhats and Uncle Elliot.

'You didn't tire the old dears out, did you?' she asked.

'Of course not,' I said, and staggered upstairs to bed.

That was my first adventure with Mrs Battyhats and Uncle Elliot. After it was over I thought things would return to normal, but of course I was wrong. I never realized at the time quite how many adventures they had.

The thing is, you could smell adventure in the air when those two were around. It was a fizzy, bubbly kind of smell and it made your nose tingle.

Sometimes I thought they were sprinkled with magic.

They were both crazy, and I loved them.

The Forbidden City

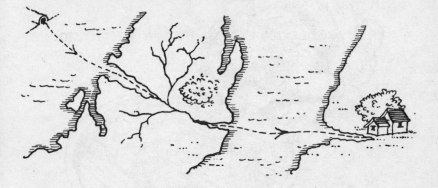

I remember the time we went off to search for two mysterious-sounding cities, the Forbidden City and the Lost City. They sounded like fabulous places but unfortunately they did not turn out to be quite what we had expected.

It all began the day Mrs Battyhats was trimming the hedges in her front garden and I was sitting on her doorstep giving advice.

We heard a hammering noise coming from under the pavement, so we lifted the

manhole cover and looked down.

Uncle Elliot was in the sewer.

'What are you up to?' we asked.

'I'm building a fantastic raft,' he said.

And indeed, Uncle Elliot's raft was
fantastic.

Crowded on to it was a cooking stove, a
small sofa, a bed, a table and a couple of
chairs.

'What do you want a raft for?' we asked.

'I'm going to sail under the city, through the sewers and then out to the seaside,' he said.

'Why?' we asked.

Uncle Elliot told us he was determined to search for the Forbidden City. Mrs Battyhats wasn't impressed. She said she had read a book about another city, one called the Lost City, and that she would prefer to look for that instead, just in case it was full of lost hats.

'It's got to be the Forbidden City,' said Uncle Elliot.

'No, the Lost City!' insisted Mrs Battyhats. She shouted so loudly down the manhole that her voice echoed through the entire sewerage system.

I could tell they were about to have a squabble, so I said, 'Why not search for them both?'

They thought this was a brilliant idea.

Mrs Battyhats packed her hats into hat boxes, locked the front door, put the cat

under a plant pot, left some milk out for the key, (she often got things the wrong way round when excited), and then squeezed herself down the manhole.

I rescued the cat and called down after them, 'Is there any room on the raft for me?'

'Of course there is,' said Uncle Elliot. 'We would love you to tag along.'

There were hundreds of sewers beneath the city. They were damp and gloomy and smelt dreadful. Me and Mrs Battyhats wore pegs on our noses because of the smell, but Uncle Elliot did not seem to mind. He had already smelt every single smell in the world.

He could sniff and tell you when there were ants about.

He could smell a grass-hopper ten feet away.

If you blindfolded him and set a firework

off, he could sniff and tell you what colour
it was.

He could even smell an elephant two
miles away if he pointed his nose in the
right direction.

Uncle Elliot used a pole to guide the raft.

He also used it to bash the rats and stop
them scrambling aboard. This upset Mrs

Battyhats, especially as rats rhymed with hats. She always said it was important to be kind to all God's creatures, but as the rats were rather nasty-looking, she pretended not to notice.

We came out of the sewer straight into the sea and immediately set off across the ocean.

Some nights, when it was cloudy, Uncle Elliot could not navigate by the stars, but he had brought along his compass and a jam jar full of glow-worms so he was able to read his charts by their light.

There was a day when we thought we would have to give up the voyage. It was when some naughty young flying-fish ripped our sail. Mrs Battyhats tried knitting a new one, but it wasn't much good, so we tied one of her hats to the mast instead. It worked perfectly.

It is hard to describe how happy I was. All my life I'd had dreams about sailing on rafts and about searching for mysterious places, and now here I was, doing both at once!

For six days and nights we were tossed about by the waves. We lived on fish and on

eggs which the seagulls laid in Mrs Battyhats's hat. She snored in the bed, Uncle Elliot snored on the sofa, and I slept on the planks in a sleeping-bag with my fingers in my ears.

And then we came to the Qwanga River. The mouth of the river was wide and full of rotting tree stumps.

'What a disgusting mouth,' said Mrs Battyhats.

'And it smells of piranhas,' said Uncle Elliot.

It was a muddy, sluggish river. In the heat of the afternoon it steamed like a saucepan full of old nappies. We drifted along and were dismayed to find that after only a mile it broke up into a number of smaller, narrower rivers. Soon we were hopelessly lost.

The river on which we found ourselves

was tiny and surrounded by jungle. Overhead were gigantic leaves shaped like elephants' ears. The sun filtered through them, casting narrow bars of greenish light upon the raft.

Mrs Battyhats complained that she was starving and was fed up with living on fish.

'Try and sniff out something unfishy,' she commanded Uncle Elliot.

He sniffed and, after a moment, declared he could smell the scent of apples. Mrs Battyhats loved apples. She insisted that we pull into the river bank and search for them.

No sooner had we begun to hack our way through the vegetation that clung to the river bank than we came to a clearing and found a low, crumbling wall overgrown with vines. We had stumbled across the outskirts of a ruined city and were standing in what appeared to be a derelict orchard.

It was full of apple trees, and the smell of apples hung over everything.

We could not make up our minds which city it was, the Lost City or the Forbidden City. Mrs Battyhats said she didn't care. All she wanted was a fat, juicy apple.

She was standing on tiptoe, about to pluck the reddest, fattest apple she could reach, when a gnarled voice screamed out, 'You can't do that!'

Through the orchard hobbled a wrinkled old man in a moth-eaten policeman's uniform.

He was the most decrepit and unlikely-looking of policemen, and Mrs Battyhats would have ignored him had it not been for the rusty blunderbuss he was waving.

'Why can't I pick just one miserable little apple?' she asked.

'Because this is the Forbidden City and it's forbidden to pick apples,' he said.

'But I'm starving,' she complained.

'It is also forbidden to starve,' he said.

Mrs Battyhats gazed up at the apples. They looked bigger and juicier with every moment that passed.

'I'll die if I don't have one,' she moaned.

'It is extra forbidden to die,' wheezed the crumpled old copper. 'If you do, I'll have to take you to jail.'

Mrs Battyhats decided he was mad. She grabbed an apple and took a massive bite from it.

The policeman didn't know what to do next. He took out his rule book and thumbed through its musty pages. 'Rule 1946, sub-section B: "It is forbidden to take criminals to prison,"' he read.

'In that case, I'll have another apple,' said Mrs Battyhats.

'And so will I,' I said.

'Me too,' said Uncle Elliot.

We shook the tree, and the apples tumbled about us.

'Is there anything that is not forbidden here?' Mrs Battyhats asked the policeman between appley munches.

'I'm forbidden to tell you,' he said.

'But why?' she insisted.

'I'm forbidden to tell you why I'm forbidden to tell you,' he said.

'This is the daftest Forbidden City I've heard about,' said Mrs Battyhats.

'I agree,' said the policeman.

'You do?' asked Mrs Battyhats in amazement.

'Oh, yes, wholeheartedly,' he said. 'But only because it is forbidden to disagree. If it was not forbidden to disagree, then I'm not sure what I'd think because thinking is forbidden, you see.'

Mrs Battyhats stomped off back towards
the raft.

'Let's go and look for the Lost City,' she snorted. 'This place will rot our brains if we stay here a moment longer.'

We loaded up with apples and followed her, leaving the old policeman behind us waving his rule book and shouting, 'It is forbidden to leave!' (But he did not try to stop us, for it was also forbidden to stay.)

We were disappointed that the Forbidden City had turned out to be such a ridiculous place, but we consoled ourselves with thinking that the Lost City might be more interesting, if only we could find it. We still had no idea which way to go, so we left everything up to the river and fate.

We sailed on through drizzle and wild, torrential monsoons. Never in my life had I imagined such a journey! Watersnakes slithered beneath us. Parrots chatted in the trees above us. We swirled around the

edges of mountains. We went down
waterfalls and rapids and through swamps
that bubbled and oozed and belched.

Sometimes the river roared, and sometimes
it murmured. It carried us faster and faster
through the jungle until finally it flung us
out into the ocean again.

The ocean was stormy now, and we were
exhausted. The only sound we could hear

was the crashing of waves, and the only scents we could smell were the scents of salty foam and apples. Darkness fell, and we tied ourselves to the raft and drifted into a deep sleep.

Uncle Elliot snored and dreamed of fabulous maps.

Mrs Battyhats snored and dreamed of fabulous hats.

I stuck my fingers in my ears and dreamed of hamburgers and milkshakes.

I woke before the others and found that the raft had come to rest against the side of an old canal. It was dark and misty, and through the mist I could make out the shapes of tall, narrow towers.

I climbed up on to the bank, and as I did so the clouds parted. Flying through them I saw what I mistook for a huge prehistoric bird. It had a long, thin body and a large

beak that tapered to a point. I was terrified
and rushed back to the raft.

'I've just seen a pterodactyl,' I whispered,
shaking Mrs Battyhats awake.

She had no idea what I meant.

'It's like a flying dinosaur,' I explained.

'Then we must be in the Lost City,' she
said.

We woke Uncle Elliot, who thought we
ought to camp on the canal bank for the
night, but as soon as we got up on to the

bank Mrs Battyhats refused to stay there, saying she thought she could see some gigantic beetles.

She also refused to leave her hat boxes behind on the raft.

'I'm not having a mischievous cave-lady come along and steal them,' she said, and clambered back down to fetch them.

We were desperate to find somewhere safe.

We tiptoed down narrow lanes and

through twisting alleyways, falling over tin cans and bags full of rubbish.

It was pitch-black and, though we could see nothing, I had the feeling that I'd been in the city before.

I finally found a place I considered safe.

And so did Mrs Battyhats.

And so did Uncle Elliot.

We were quite near each other, but we all insisted that the places we had found were the safest, and so we made three separate camps.

In the morning we discovered we had all been right, and each of us was camping in the loveliest, safest place in the world.

Without realizing it, we had come full circle, and we were camping in our own back gardens!

'I knew this was the safest place to be,' I cried.

'I knew this was the safest place!' cried Uncle Elliot.

'And I knew *this* was!' cried Mrs Battyhats. 'Now let's make some breakfast,' she said. 'We can search for the Lost City another time. After all, it's been a fabulous adventure, and that's what counts.'

The Best Hat in the World

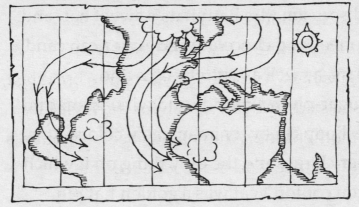

I looked out of my window one morning and saw Mrs Battyhats leaping up and down in her garden. She was waving a letter and seemed very excited.

'I've been invited to give the annual talk to the Hat Society,' she told me. 'It's a great honour, but I can't decide which hat to wear.'

'You must wear the one covered in sweets,' I said.

'You are absolutely right!' she cried, and rushed inside to fetch it.

There were lemon drops and liquorice allsorts on Mrs Battyhats's sweet hat, and toffees and chocolate and American candy bars, as well as butterscotch and sugar-plum almonds and wine-gums and lollipops in every imaginable colour. It was very large, and the only thing on it which you couldn't eat was a golden hat pin.

Mrs Battyhats came back out wearing her hat. She was very proud of it, so you can imagine her dismay when a fierce gust of wind suddenly snatched it from her head and carried it up into the sky.

Mrs Battyhats was aghast. She quivered and moaned, 'No other hat will do! I must wear that one!'

We went to Uncle Elliot's house to see if he could help us.

There was a notice pinned on his door. 'Gone to Scotland to find the Loch Ness Monster. Back Tuesday,' it read.

'But my talk is on Monday,' cried Mrs Battyhats, 'and I must get my hat back by then.'

Mrs Battyhats had a spare key to Uncle Elliot's house, so we went up to the attic where he kept maps and books full of fantastic information. We found what we were looking for beneath a book on ocean currents.

It was a map that charted the directions of all the different winds in the world. Uncle Elliot had drawn it himself. By calculating the date and time, we discovered the wind that had snatched Mrs Battyhats's hat was none other than the dreaded Wig-and-Hat-Snatching Wind and that it blew everything it stole into the Sahara Desert.

'That's that, then,' I sighed, folding away the map. 'We'll never find it now – it's impossible.'

'Jimmy Tag-along, I'm ashamed of you!' admonished Mrs Battyhats. 'If there is one thing you should have learnt from being with Uncle Elliot and myself, it is that nothing, absolutely nothing, is impossible!'

She grabbed my hand, and we dashed out of the house to Victoria Station, where she bought two tickets for the Marrakesh Express.

After the most exhausting train ride of

my life we arrived at the edge of the Sahara Desert.

We spent the day riding across the baking hot sands on the backs of camels. We lived on dried apricots and dates, and drank stale water from water bags made of goatskin. There was no sign of the hat, but we were determined to find it.

Towards evening we rested in the shadow of a ruined fort. It had long been abandoned. Its doors had crumbled away, and all its rooms were silent and covered in sand. We were wondering whether to separate and search in different directions when we saw a man crawling towards us.

He told us a miracle had happened.

'I was burning to death in the middle of the desert,' he said. 'I was without shade or water when suddenly a huge hat fell from the sky. I sheltered under it from the noonday heat. It saved my life.'

Mrs Battyhats was delighted. 'That must have been my hat,' she said. 'Where is it now?'

The man said the wind had snatched it away again and blown it deep into Africa.

'We must follow it,' said Mrs Battyhats, and so we did.

There was a terrible drought in Africa. The people were poor and very hungry, so

we were surprised when we met a group of
children who smiled and told us something
lovely had happened.

'A huge hat fell from the sky,' they said.
'It was covered in sweets. We had never
tasted anything like them before. We ate
every single one.'

Mrs Battyhats was delighted a second
time. 'That must have been my hat,' she
said. 'Where is it now?'

The children said that the moment they
had eaten the very last sugar-plum, the
wind had snatched the hat away again.

'It blew towards the ocean,' they said.

When we arrived at the ocean we met a
sailor who said a most amazing thing had
happened.

'My boat was sinking miles from land,
and I was convinced I was going to drown,'
he said. 'But suddenly a large hat fell from

the sky. I was able to climb into it and drift
ashore.'

He told us there had been a golden hat
pin in the hat which he had bent and used
as a fish-hook.

Mrs Battyhats was delighted a third time.
'That must have been my hat,' she said.

'Where is it now?'

The sailor said that as soon as he reached land a freak whirlwind came and snatched up the hat. 'It was carried off into the sky and could be anywhere by now,' he said.

I remembered reading in the newspapers that there were lots of whirlwinds in America, and it seemed a good idea to search there.

We had very little time left before Mrs Battyhats was due to give her talk to the Hat Society. We were hundreds and hundreds of miles from home, but it was unthinkable to give up after looking so hard, so we sold our camels and used the money to buy tickets on a tramp steamer bound for America.

In Texas we met an astronaut who said something fantastic had happened.

'My space shuttle had broken down,' he

said, 'and I was stranded on the moon. I
thought I would be there for ever but then,
among the moon rocks, I found an
extraordinary hat. I used it as a parachute
and floated back down to earth.'

Mrs Battyhats was delighted a fourth
time. 'That must have been my hat,' she
said. 'Where is it now?'

The astronaut said he had left it on the spot where he'd landed. 'I fell to earth in England,' he said, 'and landed in a peculiar garden where all the bushes had been clipped into the shapes of hats.'

'Why, that's my garden!' exclaimed Mrs Battyhats, and although she was relieved to have found out where the hat was at last, she thought it was hardly worth hurrying home.

'There's less than a day left before I'm due to give my talk. We'll never make it back in time,' she said.

I reminded her of what she had told me

about how nothing was impossible. And when I told the astronaut our problem, he said it would be an honour to whizz us back home.

The hat was in the garden, just as he'd said.

But of course it was now battered and crumpled and dusty and torn. All the sweets had gone, as well as the golden hat pin. It was a very miserable-looking hat now, and certainly not the kind of hat one would be expected to wear when giving a speech to the Hat Society.

There was no time left for Mrs Battyhats to repair it. She had only five minutes before she was due to give her talk.

'Quickly,' I said, 'choose another hat.'

'Certainly not,' said Mrs Battyhats. 'I shall wear this one.'

I could say nothing to dissuade her.

We arrived at the Hat Society with only a moment to spare. The hall was full of famous people, and they were all wearing exquisite hats.

When Mrs Battyhats marched up on to the stage to give her talk, they sniggered and snorted and whispered and nudged one another. They said things like, 'Surely that can't be the famous Mrs Battyhats, not with that rag on her head?'

Mrs Battyhats stood in the spotlight and, instead of giving the talk she had planned, she told them the amazing story of the hat.

She spoke of the different ways in which it had helped people and of all the remarkable places it had been to.

The audience were spellbound. There were gasps of admiration, and when she had finished her talk, they clapped and cheered and stomped their feet and said what a glorious hat it was.

The Chairwoman of the Hat Society ordered a glass case to be made for the hat, and it was put on a pedestal by the entrance, so that everybody could see how stupendous it was.

It was agreed that Mrs Battyhats had given the best-ever talk in the history of the Hat Society, and they wanted her to give another talk as soon as possible. It was even rumoured that she was going to be made Honorary President.

Mrs Battyhats was delighted with the

way things had turned out. On our way home we visited a dozen sweet shops and she bought seventy-three different varieties of sweets. She had decided to start making another hat right away.

'It's going to be even more delicious than the first one,' she said.

Mrs Battyhats Goes on Holiday

Mrs Battyhats was in the garden, watering one of her hats.

'I'm fed up with adventures,' she said. 'What I need is a nice ordinary holiday.'

'Let's go to Spain then,' suggested Uncle Elliot. 'You can lie on the beach and absolutely nothing will happen.'

'That's exactly the kind of holiday I want,' she said, 'and we can take Jimmy Tag-along with us. I'm sure his Mum won't mind.'

And, of course, Mum didn't mind – she

was glad to see the back of me for a few days.

As soon as Mrs Battyhats had decided which hats to pack, we all went to Heathrow Airport and caught an aeroplane to Spain.

The moment we landed, Uncle Elliot said he wanted to explore the mountains. Mrs Battyhats refused. She was determined to have an ordinary holiday, so she went to the hotel where she unpacked her precious hat boxes, put on her sun hat and bikini and went straight to the beach. I loved the beach, so I tagged along with her.

Mrs Battyhats said she wanted to lie down by the waves, and so she borrowed my Li-lo and marched down to the water.

'You might think I'm bit dull, wanting to snooze away, but sometimes it is important to do absolutely nothing,' she said.

I couldn't think of anything worse than doing absolutely nothing, but that's what she wanted to do, so I let her get on with it.

She rubbed on some sun-tan oil, put on a pair of sunglasses and then settled down for a snooze.

A little later, when I looked up from building a sandcastle, she had vanished.

At the time I had no real idea what had happened to her. It was only later I learnt the details.

Mrs Battyhats had fallen into a deep sleep on the Li-lo, and when she woke she found she was floating about in the Arctic Ocean,

the Li-lo having been carried there by the ocean currents.

Everything was glittery-cold and icy, and she had a foreboding that it wasn't going to be an ordinary holiday after all.

She was proved right when the Li-lo was punctured by the periscope of a passing submarine.

To avoid drowning she jumped on to the back of a whale and when the whale began to dive, she jumped on to an iceberg.

She was livid. She had wanted a peaceful holiday, and now here she was, leaping about from whales to icebergs like a demented kangaroo.

She clung to the slippery iceberg for two hours before being rescued by a gang of polar bears. She explained what had happened, but when she described how, only a few hours ago, she had been lying on a sandy beach full of half-naked people eating ice-creams, they thought she was mad.

'What she needs is a warm glass of polar bear grog,' they said, and took her along to the Polar Bear Disco.

It was a gigantic igloo full of polar bears and walruses and penguins dancing and having a fantastic time.

Mrs Battyhats drank three glasses of polar bear grog, which made her very woozy. Then she joined in the dancing.

She was a smashing dancer.

She tangoed with a polar bear.

She shimmied with a walrus.

She rock-and-rolled with a sea-lion.

And then the Abominable Snowman rushed in. He was a real spoil-sport.

He was called the Abominable Snowman because he was utterly disgusting. He had green teeth, dirty fingernails and pimples

on his chilblains. He was also very hairy and smelt rotten. He had not had a wash since finishing his last bar of soap fifty-three years before.

He grabbed hold of Mrs Battyhats with sticky fingers and slithered her off to his hidey-hole in the North Pole, where he immediately squeezed his feet into a pair of filthy dancing pumps and sneered, 'You'll have to stay here until you teach me how to dance.'

Of course, I knew none of this at the time. I was still on the beach in Spain, rushing about sick with worry. I guessed Mrs Battyhats had been carried out to sea on the Li-lo and was desperate to find Uncle Elliot and tell him.

I suddenly saw him strolling along towards me with his Emergency Bag slung over his shoulder.

I rushed up to him and blubbered, 'I think Mrs Battyhats has –'

'– probably been carried out to sea on a Li-lo,' he said, finishing my sentence.

'How do you know?' I gasped.

'Because it is impossibly impossible for

Mrs Battyhats to have an ordinary holiday,'
he sighed, with a hint of envy in his voice.
'I've never known a day when adventures
weren't absolutely buzzing around that
remarkable woman. Now stop blubbering,'
he said. 'We'll find her.'

I felt much more hopeful. Uncle Elliot
seemed to know exactly what to do.

Within a minute he had hired a wind-

surfing board. Two minutes later he had
learnt how to use it, and within three
minutes we were speeding off across the
water in search of Mrs Battyhats.

We searched in green lagoons and on

coral reefs. We peered into gloomy caves at the bottom of cliffs. We wind-surfed into bays and up estuaries. But she was nowhere to be found.

We had nearly given up hope of finding her when a submarine surfaced in front of us and the captain came up on to the deck.

'Are you two people real?' he asked,

looking down at us.

'Positively,' said Uncle Elliot.

'How about the surf-board – is *that* real?' he asked.

I told him it was.

'Thank goodness,' he said. 'You see, I'm afraid I'm suffering from a bout of subsanity. We all get it in submarines, you know. Only last week the cook imagined he was a sardine and insisted that we either eat him or feed him to the sub's cat. Of course, we did nothing of the kind. We simply put him in a large tin and left him on a shelf. Now it's my turn to imagine things.'

'What kind of things?' we asked.

'You won't believe this,' he said, 'but just now I was in the Arctic, and when I looked through my periscope I imagined I saw a fat old lady in a sun hat and a bikini. She was standing on the back of a whale, shaking her fist at me. Sheer madness, of course.'

It was the only clue we needed! Within a day we had tracked Mrs Battyhats down to the Polar Bear Disco and discovered she had been kidnapped.

We thought the polar bears were a really cowardly lot.

'Why on earth didn't you try and rescue her?' we asked.

'It's impossible to get near the Abominable Snowman – he smells so disgusting,' they said. 'Just you try. You'd probably both faint before you got within three feet of him.'

The polar bears explained that, deep down inside, the Abominable Snowman was abominable only because he couldn't dance.

'He gets furious and nasty because no one invites him to dances,' they said.

'If Mrs Battyhats has not taught him to dance within a few days, he'll boil her up and make her into soup,' said a walrus.

'That's disgusting,' said Uncle Elliot.

'Actually, it's quite nice soup,' said the walrus.

We had no time to stand around arguing about soup.

Uncle Elliot rummaged through his Emergency Bag to see if there was anything useful inside it.

He brought out a snorkle, a tent pole, a

ping-pong ball, three snowshoes, an ice pick, a length of rope and a rubber flipper.

We put on the snowshoes and the rubber flipper and swept everything else back into the bag. Then we set out to rescue our friend.

The snow had covered the Abominable Snowman's footprints, but we had no trouble tracking him. Even in the frosty atmosphere Uncle Elliot could smell the terrible pong the Abominable Snowman left trailing behind him.

We slipped and shivered and shuddered across the frozen ice. Sometimes we used sledges and were pulled along by huskies, and at other times we rode on the backs of reindeer.

At night we often made camp beneath ice-capped mountains that glittered pink in the Arctic sunset, and when the sun had vanished we sat huddled around fires. In the darkness beyond the flames I could hear the howling of Arctic wolves, but I was not scared. I was with Uncle Elliot, and I felt safe.

One morning we woke up to find that the ice on which we had camped had split away from the land. We were marooned, and it

was two days before the chunk drifted back and formed part of the coast again.

'We're bound to be too late!' croaked Uncle Elliot. 'By now the Abominable Snowman will have made her into soup and slurped her up.'

Uncle Elliot wept and I wailed, and we cursed ourselves for not being able to find her in time. We told each other about all the terrible things we were going to do to the monster when we found him.

However, when we finally reached the Abominable Snowman's hide-away nothing was as we had expected it to be.

The Abominable Snowman had not slurped Mrs Battyhats into oblivion.

He had stopped picking his nose and scratching himself. He had even had a wash, and combed his hair, and swept all his human soup bones into a corner.

Mrs Battyhats had taught him to dance, and he wasn't abominable any more!

She was delighted to see us, but the

Abominable Snowman wasn't. He did not want her to leave. He had fallen in love with her and said she looked lovely in her sun hat and bikini. He wanted her to stay for ever.

Mrs Battyhats said she did not have time to stay for ever and had to go. The Abominable Snowman nearly became abominable again when he thought we were all going to leave without him.

'I want to come to Spain and dance!' he yelled.

His heart was set on it, so we had to take him.

There was no way we could all fit on to the wind-surfer, and as there was not enough wood to build a boat, we used Uncle Elliot's ice pick to chip out four ice canoes from an iceberg.

Then we set off.

The Abominable Snowman was excited
to be coming to Spain. He sang abominable
songs and told abominable jokes.

'What's Spain like?' he asked.

We forgot that nobody had told him.

'It's hot,' we said.

'What's hot?' he asked.

'Like warm,' we said, 'only hotter.'

The Abominable Snowman did not like
the idea of things being hot, but still he

paddled along beside us.

The nearer we got to Spain, the hotter and stickier he became, until suddenly he shouted out, 'I can't stand it! I hate the hot!'

He gave Mrs Battyhats a big abominable kiss on the cheek and, with big abominable tears in his eyes, he turned his canoe around and wished us farewell.

Soon he was no more than an abominable dot on the horizon.

The canoes melted before we arrived back in Spain, but by then we had been joined by a family of dolphins, and they helped us ashore.

It was dark on the beach. The sky was littered with stars, the brightest of which was the Pole Star.

'That's the star the Abominable Snowman will be dancing under tonight,' sighed Mrs Battyhats. 'I do hope he is happy.'

The rest of the holiday was ordinary enough. I built sandcastles, Mrs Battyhats bought lots of Spanish hats and Uncle Elliot went off exploring again.

We bought a postcard, which we all signed and sent to the Abominable Snowman. Then we went home, and I wondered how long it would be before we had another adventure.

It wasn't long.